Itty ♔ Bitty PRINCESS Kitty

7

Welcome to Wagmire

by Melody Mews   illustrated by Ellen Stubbings

LITTLE SIMON

New York London Toronto Sydney New Delhi

LITTLE SIMON

An imprint of Simon & Schuster Children's Publishing Division
1230 Avenue of the Americas, New York, New York 10020
First Little Simon paperback edition February 2021. Copyright © 2021 by Simon & Schuster, Inc.
All rights reserved, including the right of reproduction in whole or in part in any form.
LITTLE SIMON is a registered trademark of Simon & Schuster, Inc., and associated colophon
is a trademark of Simon & Schuster, Inc. For information about special discounts for bulk
purchases, please contact Simon & Schuster Special Sales at 1-866-506-1949 or
business@simonandschuster.com.
The Simon & Schuster Speakers Bureau can bring authors to your live event. For more
information or to book an event contact the Simon & Schuster Speakers Bureau at
1-866-248-3049 or visit our website at www.simonspeakers.com.
Designed by Laura Roode. The text of this book was set in Banda.
Manufactured in the United States of America 0221 MTN 10 9 8 7 6 5 4 3 2
Cataloging-in-Publication Data is available for this title from the Library of Congress.
ISBN 978-1-5344-8346-0 (hc)
ISBN 978-1-5344-8345-3 (pbk)
ISBN 978-1-5344-8347-7 (eBook)

Contents

Chapter 1 Another Dragon   1

Chapter 2 A Royal Invitation   9

Chapter 3 Flying in Style   21

Chapter 4 Welcome to Wagmire!   33

Chapter 5 Pip's Palace   47

Chapter 6 Itty's First Dragon Ride   57

Chapter 7 Pip's Best Friends   69

Chapter 8 Top Secret Means Top Secret! 81

Chapter 9 Kitty with a Plan   91

Chapter 10 The Hero Princess   105

Another Dragon

Princess Itty stood on the highest perch in the royal climbing room. The floor was a long way down! But Itty wasn't going to take one big jump. No, she was going to carefully plot a course and jump from one perch to another until she reached the ground. It was a new technique she had been practicing with her mom, the Queen of Lollyland. While Itty's dad, the King, liked to take one big leap—and land with one big *thump!*—her mom preferred

to work her way down by expertly
jumping from one level to the next.
It took a lot of skill, but it was the
best and safest technique for a kitty
with small paws like Itty.

A flash of movement outside caught Itty's attention. There was a dragon heading toward the palace! Actually, he was *rolling* toward the palace, because he was wearing roller skates.

A dragon on roller skates could only mean one thing!

Itty forgot all about being careful and leaped all the way down to the ground. She landed on the floor with a *thump!* She shook her paws and raced out of the climbing room.

"Mom! Dad! An announcement dragon from Wagmire is here!" Itty yelled as she raced through the grand hallway.

Her parents were already waiting at the palace doors.

"I know it's exciting, darling, but please don't run indoors. Or shout," the Queen reminded her gently.

"Sorry, Mom," Itty replied. But from the smile on the Queen's face, Itty knew her mom wasn't upset. After all, it wasn't every day that an announcement dragon showed up!

A Royal
Invitation

The palace doors swung open. Itty recognized the announcement dragon immediately—he had come to the palace before. The last time the royal family of Wagmire visited, it had taken Itty and the puppy prince, whose name was

Pip, a while to like each other. But by the end of the visit they were great friends!

"Did Prince Pip send you?" Itty asked.

Instead of replying to Itty, the dragon unfurled the scroll he was holding, cleared his throat, and began to sing.

"Princess Itty, you may be wondering why I am here. I have been sent by the royal family of Wagmire! They wish to extend an invitation to visit their great nation. Wagmire will host a grand cel-e-bration! Oh, Princess Itty, what will you doooooo?"

The dragon took a deep bow and handed the scroll to the King.

"Itty, what do you think?" her dad asked.

"Oh!" Itty realized that the dragon was waiting for her to accept the invitation.

"Can I go?" she asked her parents.

"Of course," her mom said with a smile. "If you'd like to, that is."

Would Itty like to visit Wagmire, see Prince Pip, and attend a fancy party?

"Tell Prince Pip I'll see him soon!" Itty exclaimed.

A few days later, Itty's best friends came over to say goodbye and to help her pack.

"Do you think you'll need all those gowns?" Esme Butterfly asked. "You're only going for two days!"

"I think she needs *more* gowns!" Luna Unicorn exclaimed, popping her head out of Itty's closet. "What if they wear gowns in Wagmire to take naps? And to eat breakfast? It might be *very* fancy there!"

"Speaking of breakfast, what's the food like in Wagmire?" Chipper Bunny asked.

"I'm really not sure," Itty admitted.

"You'd better pack some snacks, just in case," Chipper advised.

Itty nodded. Her friends always had the best ideas.

"Here you go, Itty!" Luna stumbled out of the closet, buried under a huge pile of gowns. "I think you should bring at least ten dresses for every day you'll be there."

Itty giggled. Maybe her friends
didn't *always* have the best ideas.

Flying in Style

A little while later, Itty was waiting on the grand lawn for her cloud to arrive. In Lollyland, everyone traveled by cloud.

It arrived right on time. It was an extra large, super fluffy cloud. Itty hugged her friends and parents, and waved goodbye to the fairies who had come to see her off.

"They'd better feed you well, Princess Itty! Or else!" shouted Garbanzo, the fairy who ran the royal kitchen.

"See you in two days!" Itty called
as she climbed onto the cloud.

Itty settled in and moments later the cloud gently drifted up and away.

As Itty made herself comfortable, she thought about the giant dog bed-copter Pip and his family had used for their voyage to Lollyland. There was a teeny part of her that wished clouds were more luxurious.

But before Itty could even finish her thought, a squishy purple cat bed appeared on the seat next to her. A grooming station appeared on her other side. And then a dining table popped up right in

front of her. The table was filled
with all of Itty's favorite snacks!

"Now *this* is what I call traveling
in style," Itty said to herself.

As she reached for a cupcake, Itty noticed that a telescope had also popped out. She peered into it. It gave her a view of the lands they were flying over! Itty saw a kingdom covered in brightly colored flowers,

an island kingdom surrounded by turquoise-blue water, and one kingdom that appeared to be made entirely of cotton candy.

I have to remember to tell Luna, Esme, and Chipper about these places, Itty thought.

Itty was about to try out the grooming station when she felt a flutter in her tummy. The cloud had begun its descent. They must be over Wagmire! Itty rushed back to the telescope to catch her first glimpse of Prince Pip's kingdom.

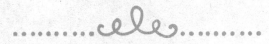

Welcome to Wagmire!

Through the telescope, Itty saw a beautiful palace surrounded by a moat. There was a big lawn with statues and trees around it. Three smaller statues stood on a red carpet in the center of the lawn. Suddenly one of the statues began

to move. Itty looked more closely.
They weren't statues after all—they
were the royal family of Wagmire!
The one jumping up and down and
waving was Prince Pip.

A few moments later Itty's cloud came to a gentle stop at the end of the red carpet. As Itty climbed out, Pip came running over.

"Welcome to Wagmire!" the King and Queen called as Pip pulled Itty in for a big hug.

"Thank you for having me as your guest," Itty replied politely, just the way she had practiced with her mom.

Itty looked up at the palace. Its sides stretched as far as her eyes could see, and when she tilted her head all the way back, she still couldn't see the tippy top of it.

"Your palace is humongous!" Itty exclaimed.

"For the next few days, this is your home," the Queen replied. "Pip, would you like to give Princess Itty the tour?"

"Oh, I have a present for you from my parents," Itty said shyly. She presented a shiny gold gift bag to the Queen. She knew what was inside—beautiful collar necklaces made from the finest silk and gems in Lollyland. Itty had promised her mom she would give the Queen the gift right away. Her mom would be so happy she had remembered!

"Oh, how wonderful," the Queen exclaimed as the King tried peeking inside the bag.

"Come on, Itty, I'll show you around," Pip said.

"Pip, I have one question for you," Itty said as they headed toward the palace entrance. "Does your palace go all the way up to the clouds?"

Pip's Palace

"Let's start the tour in the most delicious place in the palace," Pip said once they were inside. "The royal kitchen!"

The royal kitchen was as bustling as the one at Itty's home, but with one big difference—the royal cooks were little green trolls!

"Who's this, Prince Pip?"

A chubby troll had waddled over to Itty and Pip.

"This is Princess Itty," Pip said. "Itty, this is Gnocchi, head of the royal kitchen."

"Pleased to meet you," Itty said. She had never met a troll before.

Gnocchi smiled very warmly. "Welcome to Wagmire, Princess Itty. We can't wait for you to taste our cooking."

"Thank you," Itty said politely.

"Where are the kitchen fairies?" Itty whispered as she and Pip walked away.

"The best cooks in Wagmire are trolls," Pip said with a shrug. "Actually, trolls are pretty much good at everything. Kind of like the fairies in Lollyland!"

Next Pip showed Itty his fetch

room. It had machines that shot tennis balls for Pip and his parents to fetch. And part of the floor was made of dirt. The fetch room reminded Itty of her climbing room. She preferred climbing to fetch, but she played with Pip for a little while. He was her host, after all.

"And this is my room," Pip said later in the tour.

"Your room is awesome!" Itty exclaimed. Pip's bed was a huge, fuzzy dog bed. He had two treat dispensers—one with bones in it and one that had chewy bacon-flavored treats. Pip offered Itty one of each, but she wrinkled her nose.

"Don't worry, Itty. There are kitty treats in your room," Pip assured her.

"Thanks! And what's in there?"
Itty asked, pointing to a big
wooden box.

"That's my toy chest," Pip
explained. "It's filled with chew
toys and pull toys."

"You chew your toys?!" Itty
exclaimed. "Pip, don't they get
ruined?"

"Yes, but the sewing trolls fix my toys whenever they need to."

Just then, the friends heard a loud bell ringing.

It was dinnertime! And from the grumble in Itty's stomach, she knew she was hungry.

Itty's First Dragon Ride

The next morning Pip knocked on Itty's door.

"Ready to go exploring?" he asked.

"I'll meet you downstairs!" Itty called from inside her closet.

A palace troll had neatly hung

up all Itty's clothes—every one
of the twenty gowns Luna had
packed. As she pawed through
the perfect rows of dresses, Itty
thought about the delicious meal
they had eaten last night. Pip

was right—trolls *were* good at everything!

She chose a simple dress that would be comfortable for exploring, got dressed quickly, and headed downstairs. After breakfast Itty and Pip went outside.

"I'll hail our dragon," Pip said.

"What for?" Itty asked.

"To *ride*!" Pip replied. "That's how we get around in Wagmire!"

"Um . . ." Itty wasn't sure what to say. "What about your dog bed-copter?"

Pip smiled as a golden dragon swooped down and landed in front of them. "Don't worry, it's fun! I promise!"

Itty took a deep breath. The dragon *looked* friendly. Itty's tummy fluttered nervously, but she wanted to give it a try.

"Okay, let's do this!" she said.

As the dragon flew up, up, and away, Itty felt her worries fly away too.

"You're right!" she exclaimed. "This is so much fun!"

"I told you!" Pip shouted.

Every now and then the dragon would swoop down so Pip could point out a special location to Itty, like his school, the busy town, and Treat Trove, which was Wagmire's version of Goodie Grove.

"Are there syrup trolls there instead of syrup fairies?" Itty asked.

"Yes," Pip replied. "You're an expert on Wagmire already!"

A few minutes later they were flying over snowcapped mountains when the dragon began to descend. Itty saw a sparkling lake

surrounded by a lush green forest.
Then she noticed two small figures
waving to them.

Pip waved back.

Itty wondered who she was
about to meet.

Pip's Best Friends

As their dragon landed softly on the grass, a hedgehog and a mouse rushed over.

"Itty, meet my best friends," Pip said. "Wally Hedgehog and Scout Mouse."

"It's very nice to meet you,

Princess Itty," Wally said shyly.

"Please call me Itty—" Itty began. Before she could finish, Scout bolted forward and gave Itty a big hug.

"Itty, I feel like we're best friends already!" Scout squealed. "Pip told us so much about you! We're so excited to meet you! Do you like Wagmire? Do you like

being a princess? What's your favorite color? Do you have best friends? Wait, of course you do! What are their names?"

"Scout gets excited easily," Pip whispered.

Itty giggled. "I *love* it here," she began, counting off on her paw as she answered all Scout's questions. "Being a princess is super fun. Tie between pink and yellow. I have three best friends and their names are Luna, Chipper, and Esme."

Itty paused. "But now *I* have a question. Where are we?"

"This," Pip said, spreading out his arms, "is Magic Mountain Lake."

"The best place in Wagmire," Wally added.

"Wow," Itty said as she looked around. She had never seen any place quite like this.

"There's something very special that we want to show you," Pip said, and they walked into the forest.

Finally, they reached a clearing

in the woods. A tall tree stood
in the center of the clearing.
A wooden ladder was propped
against it.

"Look up," Pip said.

Itty squinted up through the branches to the top of the tree. "Is that . . ." She climbed a few rungs of the ladder to get a better look. "Is that a *tree house?*"

"It's our top secret clubhouse!" Pip said proudly.

Itty had never seen a clubhouse, let alone a *top secret* one.

"Can I see it?" she asked.

"No way, Itty!" Scout shouted. Before Itty could react, Scout burst out laughing. *"Of course*, you can see it! Let's go!"

♥ chapter 8 ♥

Top Secret Means Top Secret!

Itty scrambled up the ladder quickly. She couldn't wait to see the clubhouse! She got there before the others.

"Wow, you're a really good climber," Wally huffed as she joined Itty. "Do they teach you that at your princess school?"

"I don't go to princess school,"
Itty explained. "I guess I'm a good
climber because I'm a cat!"

A few minutes later Pip and
Scout joined them.

"Do you like our top secret clubhouse?" Scout asked excitedly.

Itty looked around. There were magic beanbag chairs to sit in, a table covered with yummy-looking snacks, piles of books and toys,

and a big window at the front of the clubhouse had a perfect view of the mountains in the distance.

Itty realized that Scout was holding her breath while she waited for Itty to reply. "I think it's wonderful!" she said quickly.

"Yay!" Scout danced around and then gave Itty another hug.

"You definitely have to meet my friend Luna," Itty said with a smile.

"Does anyone want some snacks?" Pip asked.

Itty, Scout, and Wally all said "I do!" at the exact same time.

Pip passed around a bowl of cheddar popcorn. Everyone was happily munching away when suddenly they heard a loud *crash!*

"Wh-what was that?" Wally asked.

CRASH!

Pip's puppy ears twitched. "I think it came from over there," he said, pointing to the clubhouse entrance.

The friends raced over and looked down. They gasped. "The ladder fell!" exclaimed Wally.

"How are we going to get down?!" Scout cried.

"Maybe someone can come rescue us?" Itty said.

But Pip shook his head. "No one knows where our clubhouse is. It's top secret, remember?"

chapter 9

Kitty with a Plan

As Itty stared down at the ground, a plan began to form in her mind. The branches were like the perches in her climbing room. She could plot a careful course and carry one friend down, and together they could put the ladder back.

Itty explained her idea.

"I'd start with that branch," she pointed to a branch that was under the clubhouse. "Then I'd leap to that branch below. Then there would be a really big jump, but I know I could make it," she finished, pointing to a branch near the bottom. "From there, I can jump to the ground."

"That sounds hard," Scout said.

"I'm a good climber," Itty replied. "I've been practicing getting down from the highest beams in my climbing room. I'm pretty sure I can do this."

"If Itty's sure, then I am too," Pip cheered. "I'll go with you!"

"Um . . ." Itty was glad that Pip believed in her, but he was too big for her to carry.

"I think I need to take Wally or Scout with me since they are smaller. . . ."

But Wally and Scout looked pretty scared. Itty wondered if they would agree.

"I'll do it," Wally said.

"No, I'll do it," Scout said. "I'm the smallest one."

Itty smiled. Her new friends believed in her.

Scout climbed onto Itty's back.
"Hold on tight," Itty said.

Then she leaped, landing
expertly on the branch below.

"You okay back there?" she
asked Scout.

"Y-y-y-es . . . ," Scout said.

"Just hang on, and we'll be fine!" Itty assured her.

Itty completed the next jump, and then it was time for the final leap to the bottom branch.

"I can't look!" Scout cried.

Itty paused. "Are you covering your eyes?"

"Y-yes . . . ," Scout replied.

"How are you holding on?" Itty asked.

"Oopsie," Scout said.

Itty felt Scout clutch the back of her dress again.

"Here we go!" Itty leaped to the bottom branch. She landed perfectly, and then took the small jump to the ground, where they landed, safe and sound. Then they put the ladder back where it belonged.

The Hero Princess

"Can I take a picture with you, Princess Itty?"

Itty smiled at the baby goat. "Sure," she said. "But call me Itty!"

It was later that evening, and all of Wagmire had come out for Itty's Welcome to Wagmire party. Wally, Scout, and Pip had told everyone about Itty's rescue mission at the clubhouse—without telling anyone where the clubhouse was, of course. All the animals wanted to meet the hero Princess Kitty. Some were even asking for her autograph!

This was the most spectacular party Itty had ever attended—and she had been to some pretty great ones in Lollyland! The ballroom was decorated in Itty's favorite colors of pink and yellow. Life-size cutouts of Itty were positioned around the floor for guests to take

pictures with. But as they learned
how friendly Itty was, most animals
just came over to ask for a picture
with the hero princess herself.

Itty's favorite thing at the party was the giant aquarium! It was filled with hundreds of colorful, exotic fish. Itty had made herself very dizzy zooming

back and forth watching the fish.

"I don't understand why kittens like chasing fish," Pip said as he joined her now.

"And I don't understand why puppies like chewing toys," Itty teased.

A penguin waiter walked by with a silver tray, and Itty helped herself to an appetizer.

"These taste exactly like my favorite tuna treats from home," Itty said. "That's the third thing I've tried that tastes just like one of Garbanzo's secret recipes!"

"Itty, that's because Gnocchi contacted Garbanzo to find out your favorite foods so we could serve them tonight," Pip explained.

"NO WAY!" Itty could not believe Garbanzo had shared his secret recipes.

Pip laughed. "I told you, trolls are good at everything. Even getting secret recipes from fairies!" Then his smile turned a little sad. "Your visit went by so fast! I'm going to miss you, Itty."

Itty returned Pip's smile. "I'm going to miss you, too," she said. And it was true. She was sad to be leaving tomorrow. But she also couldn't wait to get home and tell everyone about her exciting adventures in Wagmire!

......ele......
Here's a sneak peek at Itty's next royal adventure!

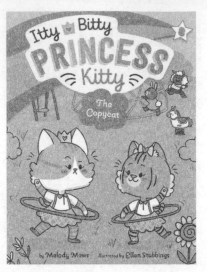

Itty Bitty Princess Kitty used a miniature hammer to lightly tap on a purple rock.

Nothing happened.

"I'm not having much luck," Itty said.

"Me neither," Luna Unicorn sighed. "But look at all *he's* got!"

Luna gestured to a panda with a gigantic pile of rocks.

Well, they weren't exactly rocks. They were rock *candy*. Itty and Luna were at Rock Candy Rocks, where the animals and other creatures of Lollyland could come and collect rock candy for themselves.

"He's smacking the rocks really hard and they're breaking into a million little pieces. Let's try doing that," Luna said.

"Well, we're not supposed to hit that hard," Itty reminded her.

"If a rock candy fairy sees—"

Just then, a rock candy fairy *did* see. She sped over, waving her arms and blowing a tiny whistle.

"Uh-oh," Luna mumbled.

"Let's find a different spot," Itty whispered.

There were many different types of Lollyland fairies, but one thing they all had in common was that they *loved* enforcing rules.